A Tale of Three Banks

Brass Tacks Publishing

Saint Paul, Minnesota

Written and illustrated by Brass Tacks Publishing, LLC
www.brasstackspublishing.com

Not so long from now,
in a town like any other...

Once upon a cloudy day,
    as gloomy as can be,
a stranger walked into the town
    of Opportunity.

His name was Tek, his step was sure,
he waved for all to see.
He'd come to show what banks could do
with new technology.

Regressive Reginald was standing
on the steps outside.
And when he caught a glimpse of Tek,
his first instinct was **hide!**

The stranger wore a big tool belt
and had a friendly grin.
But Reginald made up his mind:
"I will not let him in!"

So Tek departed, feeling sad
and trying not to frown.
He hoped he would have better luck
with other banks in town.

And Reginald sat down and sighed,
afraid his bank would fail.
He felt convinced that ROI
was just a fairy tale.

Another opportunity would
very soon commence,
when Tek approached Complacent Carl
sitting on a fence.

So Carl stayed upon his fence,
not sure what he should do.
And Tek decided that he'd have to
look for someone new.

The helpful stranger then continued
walking down the street.
It wasn't long before he came
upon Progressive Pete.

A few years later, things had changed;
    of this there was no doubt.
The flowers started blooming, and
    the sun at last came out!

When Tek returned, he saw one bank
was filled up to the brim.
Progressive Pete was doing great;
his customers **loved** him!

And so each banker chose his fate.
Our story is now through.
What kind of banker will **you** be?
The choice is up to you!

The End.

CFC Technology un-complicates growth for
financial institutions (FIs) through the intelligent
use and deployment of technology. Our approach to
capture, compliance, and computing solutions allows
FIs to choose tailored, on-site or cloud-based
technologies. By keeping pace with rapidly changing
technology trends, we help community banks and
credit unions deliver leading-edge solutions
that create and foster strong business relationships.

For more information, please visit our website:
www.cfctechnology.com